KU-008-071

Sir Gawain and the Green Knight

A free translation for contemporary readers

Sir Gawain and the Green Knight

A Christmas Tale from long ago

Margaret Isaac

Illustrations
Barbara Crow

APECS PRESS ∆ CAERLEON

Published by
APECS Press
Caerleon
Wales UK

Editing, design and typesetting by
APECS Press Caerleon

ISBN 0 9537267 4 6

Printed by Keith Brown & Sons Ltd, Cowbridge

By the same author

Tales of Gold

Stories of Caves, Gold and Magic.

Nia

The story of growing friendship between a boy and a girl set against the backdrop of the legend of Llyn-y-Fan Fach.

Teaching Story in the Primary School (1)

(Language resources for Key Stage 1 based on the story 'The Owl Who Was Afraid of the Dark' by Jill Tomlinson).

Language Learning through Story (1)

(Language resources for Key Stage 2 based on the story 'Tales of Gold' by Margaret Isaac).

Language Learning through Story (2)

(Language resources for Key Stages 2 and 3 based on the story 'Nia' by Margaret Isaac).

Forthcoming publications

A Strange Birthday

A story about a little boy who is asthmatic and who wants to spend his fifth birthday at home rather than in hospital.

The Broken Bracelet

A ghostly tale of intrigue and suspense about a Roman talisman.

Language Learning through Story (3)

(Language resources for Key Stages 2 and 3 based on the story Gawain and the Green Knight translated by Margaret Isaac).

Welsh language translations of all publications.

To

E J Llewellyn

Who taught me to love the poem

CONTENTS

FOREWORD

The story "Sir Gawain and the Green Knight" has a gripping plot, with a series of unfolding clues which lead new readers to a surprise ending. Characters leap out amid vivid passages of narrative description to stir our senses into action – the true response of readers to a well-defined story.

The author has broken new ground in this tale by giving us a contemporary version of an enthralling medieval story.

As in her previous writings, the author opens up new landscapes for the reader to view and ponder. Qualities of human frailty and strength witnessed in this free translation of a fourteenth century poem have much relevance in today's society. Sir Gawain, the youngest and most innocent of King Arthur's knights, shows how the moral code of his time enables him to demonstrate courage in adversity. The many unseen dangers and temptations facing our hero are no less real today. Could we not take a lesson from Gawain?

This enchanting story is highly entertaining while giving us much food for thought.

Molly Rees

Formerly primary school teacher and advisory teacher Dyfed LEA. Presently, a freelance scriptwriter for BBC Wales.

INTRODUCTION

IN this story of illusion, nothing is as it seems, from the beheading of the Green Knight within the first few pages of the story to the meeting at the mysterious green chapel at the end.

The character of Gawain is cast in heroic tradition. His unique characteristic is that of courtesy, a virtue incorporating the good manners and behaviour expected of a true knight of King Arthur's court.

As befits a hero, Gawain defeats monsters, battles against cold and hunger, and finally faces death itself at the hands of the Green Knight. But in this story of illusion, such dangers are easy to recognise. The temptations inside the castle are more dangerous because the hero is off his guard and unaware of the peril he is facing. In fact his knighthood is being severely tested during his meetings with the lady when they are alone and the lord is away on hunting expeditions.

When Gawain resists the temptations of the lady of the castle, he is unwittingly passing the greatest of tests. His own chivalric code, representing the courtly way of life, is being tested by the lady on behalf of the lord.

The later confrontation at the green chapel with the Green Knight has already been decided by Gawain's earlier behaviour towards the lady. The real victory has taken place in the illusory world of the lord's castle, and Gawain's innate courtesy has saved him from death. He has also justified the world to which he belongs, that of the Arthurian court which was challenged by the Green Knight.

The symbolism of the story clothes a deeper truth. Gawain represents youth and energy, life itself. If he fails the tests, not only he will die, everything he represents will die too. He represents the virtues of courage, endurance and Christian charity, so that if he is defeated, winter will remain for ever, there will be no spring and therefore no life.

At the Green Chapel, Gawain comes face to face with death itself, and, as in all the best tales, good overcomes evil.

The character of the Green Knight is full of ambiguities. He is menacing, pagan, uncivil, robust, strong, and courageous. He also possesses supernatural powers which appear to give him the upper hand in the confrontation between himself and Gawain.

His strongest card is that of deceit. He is playing with an open deck of cards in front of him, Gawain is playing blind. Gawain's strongest cards are his innocence and goodness. In playing a game with Gawain, the Green Knight displays a kind of humour and often seems to be enjoying a joke at Gawain's expense. But the game is deadly serious. The Green Knight is challenging the way of life symbolised by the court of King Arthur, a way of life which is civil and Christian, and represents goodness and life.

The ambiguity of the character of the Green Knight is partly explained by the revelation that the challenge to the court of King Arthur comes from Morgan le Fay who has placed the Green Knight under an enchanted spell to do her bidding. If Gawain fails, the Green Knight will also die! He too therefore shows courage.

So the illusion is maintained to the last page. The story teller has given many clues and the end is full of surprises, yet it is not unexpected to the alert reader. Perhaps it is Gawain who has the last laugh!

Margaret Isaac

A MARVEL AT KING ARTHUR'S COURT

T was Christmas time in the court of King Arthur. The Great Hall was alive with the bustle and jostle of the festive season.

Richly decorated tapestries hung on the stout stone walls. The high table was set on a platform, and was adorned with rich silk hangings brought from France. Over it hung a canopy of fine tapestry made of heavy linen embroidered with many precious jewels, which the knights had brought back from the Crusades in the East.

Each knight had a pennant which bore his special emblem; these pennants were fixed behind the chairs on which the knights sat, proudly proclaiming the courage of their owners. Arthur's was the most splendid, with a large red dragon emblazoned in the centre.

Other members of the royal household were seated at two wooden benches placed at each corner of the high table. The great festive board groaned under the weight of capons cooked in delectable sauces, huge venison pies covered with rich golden pastry and wild boar roasted to perfection.

Servants bustled hither and thither tempting lords and ladies with sweetmeats of every description or offering goblets of rich red wine and foaming beer.

Colourful jesters entertained the guests with amazing juggling feats and breathtaking somersaults.

The assembled company were indeed in happy, festive mood.

Arthur, young and boyish looking, was flushed from the games and the excitement of the last few days' festivities.

He spoke to the gentle Elaine as he watched his graceful wife Guinevere chatting with Launcelot. Gawain, Arthur's nephew, attended courteously to Gwenhwyfach, Arthur's sister-in-law, while Gawain's sister, Gwyar, listened to the conversation between Owain and his sister Morfudd.

Gawain's mother, Morgause, talked earnestly to Merlin, while Morgan le Fey, Arthur's stepsister, listened closely to her son Mordred, who appeared to be flushed with anger over some imagined slight from one of the assembled company.

Menw sat near Kay, who raised his glass to the wise enchanter, while the great poet Llywarch Hen gazed into the distance, deep in thought.

Arthur rose to his feet, his goblet of wine in his hand. A hush descended on the assembled company.

The young king looked at his guests with pride and affection.

"My friends," he said, "Christmas is a time of miracles and magic. We have enjoyed splendid entertainment during the last few days." A murmur of assent came from the guests. "But I have a great desire to witness a greater spectacle, some great miracle."

His illustrious guests looked at each other in some bewilderment. What, they wondered, could surpass the entertainment they had enjoyed over the last few days.

Arthur looked around expectantly. There was silence. Then, there was a sound as of rushing wind and a great clatter as the door of the great hall burst open!

The first thing the knights were aware of was a mighty rattling of hooves. They saw a knight of immense size thrusting forward a huge horse. He halted sharply in front of the great king.

Arthur looked up at the fearsome sight!

A man towered above him, easily twice as big as any knight sitting there. This might have astonished the king and his company, but the overwhelming spectacle was the colour of this giant and his horse. They were both green all over!

The Green Knight wore a short green tunic, a green fur trimmed cloak and green stockings. Even his long hair and his great bushy beard were green!

His green horse wore a green cloth on its back and the bridle shone with green gems.

Although the giant was a fearsome spectacle, the weapon he carried in his hand was even more terrifying. It was a huge, shining, fearsome axe. In his other hand he carried a cluster of red-berried holly.

Is it any wonder that the company seated in the great hall were silent!

The Green Knight looked around at the assembled company:

"Well," he boomed, his voice resounded through the hall, "so this is Arthur's Court! I am told, Sir King, that your knights are the bravest in the land. We shall see."

His voice was mocking. "You are looking for a Christmas game. I throw down this challenge!

Anyone of you may strike me anywhere and as hard as you like with one blow. I will stand quietly and accept the blow without flinching, but he must agree to allow me to strike the same blow in the same manner a year and a day hence."

He paused. The knights looked at each other. They thought, "We could kill him quite easily with one blow from that shining axe he holds in his hand." But they were uneasy. The challenge came too easily, there was something sinister about the strange man. Surely he would not issue such a challenge if he didn't have some magic within him. They were sure there was some deception behind his words. There was silence.

"Well," he said tauntingly, "this is what I expected. Arthur's knights are supposed to be the most courageous and honourable in the world, yet no-one will accept a challenge which allows them to strike a blow against a man who is prepared to stand without retaliating. What cowards! But I'm not really surprised."

He laughed loudly at their consternation and Arthur turned quite pale with shame.

Angrily the king said:

"You are speaking very foolishly, but I am quite prepared to accept your reckless challenge. Hand me your axe."

Arthur took the great weapon in both hands, swung it around him, feeling its weight and preparing himself for striking the Green Knight. But at that moment, the sound of Gawain's voice, made the heroic king hesitate:

"My lord king," said Gawain, "I beg you to let me take up this fight. Of all the brave men in this company, I am the least wise and the weakest, if I lost my life it would be of little consequence. I ask you to grant my request because I am your nephew and the same blood runs in our veins."

Arthur looked at Gawain with fondness and pride, "Take up the challenge with my blessing," he said, as he handed him the weapon, "but be sure to settle the matter with the first blow, you must not risk retaliation from such a man."

While the two men had been speaking, the Green Man eyed Gawain curiously:

"What is your name?" he asked.

"I am called Gawain," the good knight replied "I accept your challenge and will strike you one blow on the conditions you make. I will meet you in a year's time and accept a return blow, but I do not expect to have to keep my side of the bargain."

The giant smiled at the noble knight:

"I am happy to accept you Sir Gawain as the man to strike me. I accept your blow on condition you promise to seek me out in one year's time, so that I may return the strike and I do expect to meet you then." He smiled mischievously.

"How will I find you?" said Gawain." I do not know your name or where you live."

"After you have struck the blow, I will tell you my name and where I live," said the huge man.

The Green Knight stood in the middle of the hall with his head bent forward so that his neck was exposed. Gawain gripped the axe firmly, raised it high, and slashed it down hard through the giant's neck so that the head fell on the floor. Yet the man did not fall! He strode forward and picked up his head, held it by the hair and pointed the face toward the high table. It lifted its eyelids, looked grimly at the guests and said:

"Now look to your promise Sir Gawain. In a year's time seek me in the Green Chapel, where you must receive from me the same stroke that you have just dealt to me. I am the Knight of the Green Chapel, find me there or be called a coward!"

After these words, he swung himself up onto his horse, and rushed out through the door, still holding his head in his hand.

What then!

Gawain and Arthur looked at each other in silent amazement. They were lost for words. Arthur had asked for a marvel and they had truly witnessed one!

At last, Arthur recovered his composure and said:

"We will hang the axe on the wall, that people may wonder at it. But now let us eat and make merry as is fitting at Christmas time."

But Gawain remained silent, thinking of the peril he had to face at the Green Chapel, a year from that day.

A Perilous Journey

ESPITE the prospect of his coming ordeal, Gawain was a good Christian knight and his faith kept him in good heart.

When the Green Knight had surprised Arthur's court, it had been deep mid-winter, when everything seemed dead, the trees without their leaves showing only their skeleton frames.

Yet, even then, there was the promise of the Spring to come. Hedgerows protected small closed buds and crocuses and snowdrops rested warmly beneath the snow, waiting to be awakened by the gentle Spring sunshine.

Soon, warmer rainshowers would awaken the flowers from their long rest, and birds would begin to chatter as they busied themselves with their nests.

Summer then turns the countryside green, hedgerows burst into life, and flowers, birds and insects come alive in the Summer sun. Flowers give birth to the fruits of Autumn, leaves turn to russet, gold and brown, and soon Winter comes again. Gawain must now prepare for his perilous quest.

As he made his plans for the journey, his friends expressed their anxiety for his safety, but he was resolute.

"The time has come for me to seek the Knight of the

Green Chapel." he said to the king. "I must start my journey and put my trust in God."

He began to make ready at dawn. His shining armour was heaped on rich red silk carpet. Maidens attended him helping him to get ready for his quest.

First they placed on him a doublet of precious silk and a beautifully embroidered tunic lined with white fur. They placed steel shoes on his feet, wrapped steel around his legs, and polished knee-pieces fastened with knots of

gold. Then they fastened thigh-pieces tied with laces and placed on him a mail shirt made with beautiful cloth and strengthened with bright steel rings.

Brightly polished arm-pieces were fixed on both his arms, with shining elbow-pieces and steel gloves.

Over his armour he wore a splendid vest of rich material, embroidered with his heraldic emblems. His spurs were made of gold, a trusty sword hung by his side and a silk sash encircled his waist.

When Gawain was fully dressed, he seemed like a sun god, and a worthy opponent of the Green Knight and the forces of darkness which threatened King Arthur and the world over which he ruled.

After he was dressed, Gawain went to church and offered prayers to God. Then he and the whole of King Arthur's Court assembled in the courtyard, where his friends got ready to take their leave of him.

Gawain's horse had also been made ready and was waiting quietly to receive his master. His horse was called Gringolet.

Gringolet, too was equipped in the most splendid apparel, with a bright gold saddle and a golden bridle, which gleamed like the sun.

Gawain picked up his helmet and put it on. It was also of gold and towered high on his head. The visor was studded with precious jewels, and on the silk borders were embroidered birds, turtles and love-knots.

He carried a shield with the pentangle in shining gold carved on its front. Gawain chose it because he knew that it had magic properties which he hoped would protect him.

Now, Gawain was ready, with a spear in his hand, so he bade them all goodbye and sallied forth.

The first part of his journey took him across the length and breadth of Britain. Throughout his travels, he had no shelter, and no friend.

He asked every stranger he met if they knew where the dwelling place of the Green Knight may be, but no-one could answer him.

As he continued his arduous journey, he struggled over mountains, waded through tempestuous rivers, and fought with monsters, dragons, wolves, and the wild trolls who lived in the mountains. He also had to battle against wild bulls and bears and even fierce ogres who pursued him high into the mountains. He needed all his strength and courage and faith in God to survive these dreadful creatures.

As if this was not enough, he also had to contend with foul winter weather. The earth was hard and bare, the water in many streams was frozen, and poor Gawain, half-dead with cold, had to sleep in his hard armour on the bare cold rocks.

Gawain continued his travels in this pitiful state throughout the year.

Finally on Christmas Eve, he felt quite desperate, and fell on his knees in prayer. He begged the Virgin Mary,

Mother of Jesus, to help him to find some shelter, then he lay down on the hard ground, as close to Gringolet as he could get, for warmth, and fell into a troubled sleep.

The next morning, as he rode through some woods, he noticed poor half-starved birds perched on the bare branches of trees. They looked cold and miserable, but even so, they tried to utter a feeble chirp.

Gawain repeated his prayer to Mary to help him find some shelter, where he hoped to seek comfort and take communion. All Christians were supposed to do this at Christmas time.

Just as he was finishing his prayer, he looked up and thought he saw a dwelling surrounded by a moat. It looked like the most beautiful castle a knight had ever seen. It stood in the centre of a ring of pointed stakes, and shimmered as though it were some kind of enchanted mirage. Then as he came nearer, he saw that it was built of hard stone with many towers, turrets and pinnacles all pointing upwards, towards the sky.

As Gawain approached the gates, he was greeted by a large, bluff looking man who turned out to be the porter of the castle.

“Good sir,” said Gawain, “will you ask the lord of this dwelling if I may find some shelter here for the night?”

“Certainly,” said the porter, “I will be glad to do so,” and he led Gawain and Gringolet across the drawbridge.

When Gawain reached the courtyard he was surprised to be greeted by a large company of knights. They seemed to know who he was, and were very friendly. “You are most welcome to the castle,” said one, “we hope you will stay and enjoy our food and shelter. You look as if you have had a rough journey.”

“I thank you from the bottom of my heart,” said Gawain, gratefully, “your hospitality is most welcome to a tired and hungry knight.”

Servants led away his horse and the knights conducted him to the great hall.

He was relieved to take off his helmet, sword and buckler and handed them to a smiling servant, who led him towards a bright warm fire.

As he warmed his hands before the cheerful blaze, the lord of the castle strode in to give him a hearty welcome.

"Gawain," he said, "you are as welcome here as if you were in your own home, please make yourself comfortable."

Gawain thanked him courteously.

The lord seemed to Gawain to be a man of enormous size. He had a ruddy complexion and a flowing reddish-brown beard and a very jovial manner.

The servants were ordered to conduct Gawain to the room where he was to stay. As he entered, he was astonished to see how wonderfully furnished it was. There were bed-curtains of finest silk and rich tapestry hanging on the walls and on the floor.

At last, Gawain was able to take off his heavy armour. He was given a rich silk gown, which felt soft and comforting after his long and arduous journey. He looked very handsome. Feeling very relaxed and comfortable, he was led back to the warm fire, near which a table was set with a fine white cloth.

He washed his hands and settled down to enjoy the delicious food they had prepared for him.

Several wonderful soups were offered, followed by fish of all kinds, baked in different ways and served in delectable sauces. Gawain thought it a feast indeed!

The people in the company politely asked him where he came from.

"My name is Gawain," he replied, "and I come from the court of King Arthur."

To his surprise, his words were greeted with loud laughter from the lord of the castle!

After the meal, Gawain and the rest of the knights present at the meal, attended evensong in their chapel, as was the custom at this time of year.

Sitting in a special pew, Gawain noticed the lady of the castle seated in her pew.

He thought she was the most beautiful lady he had seen, even more beautiful than Queen Guinevere.

Sitting by her side was another lady, but whereas the young lady was beautiful, the other was old, and withered!

The young lady wore a beautiful silk gown adorned with jewels, showing her soft white shoulders and throat.

The old one was muffled to the eyes with scarves and veils and was dressed in black. All one could see of her were black brows, two small eyes, a protruding nose and a grim mouth. She was short and stumpy and squat, whereas the young lady was tall, slim, graceful and comely.

Gawain knew which one he preferred!

He bowed courteously to the old woman, then embraced the young lady and kissed her hand.

After evensong, everyone returned to the great hall where the lord of the castle entertained

Gawain throughout the evening with many festive games.

Gawain stayed with this company for three days, feasting and making merry. On the the third day, the other guests began to depart.

Gawain too began to make preparations to leave, mindful of his quest to seek the Knight of the Green Chapel. However, the lord of the castle, begged him to stay a little longer. "I would like to hear more of your adventures, and how you came to find this place."

Then Gawain told him about the challenge of the Green Knight.

"I must seek him out at the Green Chapel," said he, "I have pledged my honour and that of the court of King Arthur, and I would rather die than fail in this quest."

Gawain was surprised again when the lord gave a loud laugh and said to him,

"You can relax here a little while. And you need not feel anxious about finding the Green Chapel. I will make you as comfortable as you wish, you may rest easy until the appointed day. When that day comes, I will tell you where the Green Chapel is, it lies not two miles from here."

Gawain was pleased to think that he had neared the end of his journey and grateful to his host for his hospitality.

Then the lord of the castle said to Gawain:

"Rest here in my dwelling and let my wife take care of you and attend to your needs. I have engaged myself to go to the hunt and must be up at dawn.

"Look here," he continued, as if he had just had a thought. "shall we have a little wager? Whatever I catch and bring back from the hunt, I will give to you, if, in exchange, you give to me whatever you may receive in my home, while I am away."

Gawain was happy to fall in with this jovial arrangement.

"Certainly," said the brave young knight, "I shall be happy to agree to your generous request."

"Then let us seal the bargain with a glass of wine," said the lord. This they did and afterwards they all retired to bed for a good night's sleep.

THE HUNT

BEFORE dawn, people were stirring, making ready for the day's hunt. The first to rise from bed was the lord himself. The horses were led into the courtyard, the kennel doors opened and the hounds called out. They began barking fiercely and chased about until they were called to order.

This magnificent company rode out into the forest, to the strident sounds of the bugle.

The wild creatures hearing this cry, quivered with fear. The deer ran in all directions seeking cover, but the lord had given orders to allow the bucks and harts to go free, because it was the close season. This meant that men were forbidden by law to disturb the male deer so that the species would not become extinct. So the men were hunting only the hinds and does.

The arrows shimmered as they were shot from the bows, sinking into the flesh of these timid creatures. They screamed as they lay dying, and those who escaped the arrows, were chased and pulled down by the hounds. The deer that had been killed were prepared for bearing home to the castle.

The lord was always in the thick of the hunt, enjoying himself hugely.

Meanwhile, Gawain, lay in his bed, sleeping peacefully. As he slumbered, he thought he heard a sound.

Peeping cautiously through the bed-curtains, to see what it may be, he saw the beautiful lady, the wife of the lord of the castle, quietly closing the door and creeping surreptitiously towards his bed.

Gawain felt embarrassed and tried to pretend to be asleep. But she continued to steal softly towards his bed, crept up close to him, and seated herself quietly by his side.

She watched him a long while, waiting for him to wake. Gawain kept his eyes closed, while he wondered what he should do. He did not wish to offend her, but he knew that he must behave chivalrously in another man's home.

"Perhaps I should find out what she wants," he decided at last, since she did not appear to be leaving. He stirred and stretched himself as though he was just waking up. Then he opened his eyes, pretended to be aware of the lady for the first time and affected surprise.

She smiled at him affectionately. "Good morning, Sir Gawain," she said, "you were so sound asleep, anyone might have entered your room and captured you. I think I shall bind you fast in your bed."

She spoke playfully.

"Beautiful lady," said Gawain, "you are mistress of the house and as a true knight I must obey you. If you would be gracious enough to allow me to get up and dress fittingly for such a kind hostess, we might continue this pleasant conversation." He was trying to maintain his good manners without offending either the lady or her husband!

"No, indeed!" said the lady, adroitly avoiding his proposal, "I shall keep you here, as you are, for to tell the truth, I admire you greatly. You are a handsome knight and I would be very happy indeed if you were my husband."

"I am flattered by the compliment you pay me, my lady," said Gawain, "but I am not worthy of the honour. If I may serve you in some other way, I would do so gladly."

She still replied that of all men, Gawain was to her the most perfect knight, and if it were possible, she would prefer him to be her husband.

"I am conscious of the honour you pay me," replied Gawain, "but I know that your lord is far more worthy than me."

She smiled and began to make her departure. Gawain was very relieved. But as she reached the door, she said:

"You know Gawain, you disappoint me, you have not behaved as a true knight should."

Gawain feared he had failed to observe the good manners of an honourable man, and might have inadvertently offended her.

"How have I disappointed you?" he asked.

"Any man of goodness and courtesy," she replied, "would not have entertained a lady in his room, as you have done, without at least one embrace to show your respect and admiration."

"That I will do gladly," said Gawain, with some alacrity. So they embraced, and the lady softly left the room.

Gawain lost no time in jumping out of bed and dressing himself quickly, just in case she should decide to return. Then he went down to breakfast.

Meanwhile the lord of the castle continued with his hunt. He and his company killed many barren does and hinds, and neatly prepared the carcases for bearing home.

The men prepared the animals efficiently and expertly. First they opened up the dead animals, then cut away the fat, and the second stomach. They hacked off the legs, stripped the hide, broke open the belly and removed the entrails.

Then they cut through the shoulder bones cleanly, leaving the sides intact, and cut the chest clean in two. They whipped out the guts, flicked out the

shoulder fillets, and ripped free the rib fillets. The spine also was cleared right down to the haunch, which they cut off.

Then they turned their attention to the thigh, freeing it of folds and hacked away to unbind the backbone. They cut off the head and neck and flung into the bushes the worthless parts for the birds to eat. Then they skewered through the flanks and hung up their booty by their legs. The lights, the liver and tripes were thrown to the hounds.

In this way they returned home and as the lord entered the hall, Gawain greeted him.

The big man ordered the venison to be brought before them and asked Gawain if he approved of the spoils.

“Certainly,” replied Gawain, “I have not seen such splendid results for many years, particularly in winter time.”

“It is yours, Gawain, according to our bargain,” said his host.

"I give you many thanks," replied the good knight, and he embraced his host, as he had similarly done to the lady. "You have now received all that I gained while you were away," he said.

"That is good," the man said, "but may I ask from whom you received the embrace?"

"I shall not tell you," replied Gawain, "because that was not part of our bargain." At this they laughed merrily and went to supper.

In the evening, by the firelight, they agreed to a similar bargain. The following day, the lord would give Gawain whatever he won in the forest, while Gawain would give in exchange what he may acquire at home in the castle.

So the great lord was up early again the next morning to make ready for the hunt. He and his companions rode into the forest, thrusting their way through thorny bushes, until they scented their prey hiding near a quagmire.

They sounded the horn and urged on the hounds who fell on the trail vigorously, making a fearful noise. The huntsmen urged them on, as the baying hounds surged between a pool and a great rock which the men quickly surrounded. They were certain that their quarry was hiding nearby. Men beat the bushes and made a great noise till a creature suddenly lunged forward, it was a fearsome boar of enormous size.

He had separated from his herd, being old and brawny and the biggest of them all.

He grunted fearsomely and thrust through the hounds, killing three instantly, then ran on unscathed. The hounds were regrouped and the men hurried after their quarry, hallooing loudly. Many times he turned and attacked the dogs and they moaned piteously from the wounds he inflicted.

Then the men loosed their arrows at him but they could not pierce his flesh; the shaft of the arrow shattered and the head rebounded off his body.

But the boar continued to be battered by unceasing blows, until he was goaded and driven mad with fear and rage. He dashed at the men, striking savagely, so that many ran for their lives in fear.

But the lord lunged after him, blowing his bugle and rallying his hounds. He pursued the wild boar until sunset.

Gawain, meanwhile, rested peacefully in his comfortable bed at home.

Again, the lady visited him in his room, trying to tempt him with her beauty. This time, as she entered the room, Gawain welcomed her immediately.

"It seems strange to me, Gawain," she said, "that such a noble knight of Arthur's Court should not behave more honourably."

"I do not understand you," he replied, "but if I have offended you, I am deeply sorry."

"When I visited you on the last occasion, you embraced me," said the lady. "According to your code of chivalry, that kiss meant that you should claim me as your own lady."

"My sweet lady," said the knight, "you should not say this. If I did claim you, and you denied me, I would have placed you in a difficult situation. You would deny me, but the fault would be mine for placing you in such a compromising position."

"You could not be denied," she said, "for if I were so ill-bred as to resist you, your strength could overcome me."

"Where I come from," said Gawain, "such a man would be ill thought of, gifts do not prosper if they are given with ill-will. I am here at your command, embrace me as you please."

So the lady leaned forward and embraced Gawain affectionately, and they spoke fondly to each other.

The lady urged Gawain to say how much he admired her beauty, but he refused to be tempted by her exhortations, however hard she tried, so she embraced him a second time and went her way.

The lord of the castle still pursued the savage boar. The fierce creature broke the backs of his best hounds, until the bowmen forced him away from them. At last the beast began to tire and tried to find refuge in a hole in a rock beside a running stream.

He stood at bay, in this crevice, with a bank protecting his back. He confronted the men, displaying his foaming mouth and wicked white tusks. No one dared go near him for he had hurt many men with those tusks. He stamped the ground with rage, glaring at his tormentors with red, blood-shot eyes.

Then the lord urged his horse forward, alighted and drew his sword. He strode boldly into the stream where the boar was standing.

The beast sprang at the man and they grappled together, but the lord thrust his sword deep into the heart of the boar driving it in up to the hilt.

Immediately the pack of hounds leapt in to the attack and seized the wild animal. The men tugged him to the shore where the dogs destroyed him.

The bugles blew triumphantly, while a skilled man began to slash open the dead animal.

First he cut off its head and hoisted it up for all to see the spoils of victory. Then he cut open the ridge along the back of the animal, brought out the intestines and cooked them on coals. Mixed with bread these would provide a tasty meal for the dogs. Then the man brought out the brawn from within the broad flanks, and finally the entrails.

He tied the two halves of the dead beast together and hung them on a strong stake. The victorious hunters started for home, bearing the head of the boar in front of the strong, brave man who had killed the savage beast.

Gawain greeted his host warmly on his return home.

The lord recounted his fierce fight with the wild boar, showing him the spoils. Gawain congratulated him on his courage. "You were undoubtedly in great danger," said he, "I am glad to see you arrive home safely."

"Thank you, Gawain, for your kind words," said the lord, "you know that these spoils now belong to you, according to our bargain."

Gawain, thanked him, embracing him twice, as he had done with the lady previously.

"You have now received all that I acquired while you were away," said Gawain.

That night they feasted, sang Christmas carols and enjoyed splendid entertainment.

While they spent the time in this way, the lord suggested that they play their game for a third time, but Gawain was conscious that the time was fast approaching when he must keep faith with the Knight of the Green Chapel.

"You have given me marvellous hospitality," he said, "but I beg that you will allow me to leave in the morning so that I can seek out the Green Chapel as I have sworn to do."

"I beg that you will stay one more night," said his host, "I swear you will find the Green Chapel on New Year's Day as I have promised. Please remain in your room and rest, while I go hunting once more.

"We will make our bargain again. Twice I have tested you and twice found you true. May I do so a third time?"

So Gawain agreed and they retired for the night.

The lord of the castle set forth early the following morning with a host of knights, in pursuit of the fox.

A small hound found the scent of the animal, and the rest of the pack rushed forward on the trail, but the cunning fox doubled back on his tracks, leapt over a ditch and crept stealthily into a valley. He thought he had deceived the dogs but he had stumbled on a tracking-station by mistake.

Three greyhounds were waiting for him and threatened to leap on him immediately. Dismayed, the fox turned and raced along a different track away into the woods with the hunt following in full cry, but he was so wily that he eluded the huntsmen till mid-morning.

In the castle, while Gawain lay sleeping, the lady dressed herself in her most beautiful gown trimmed with finest fur, revealing her lovely white throat and soft shoulders. Her long fair hair was dressed with the most precious jewels.

She came into the bedroom, threw open the window and called out to the knight,

"Why Gawain, how soundly you sleep! Look how brightly the sun shines!"

Her words roused Gawain who had been dreaming of his perilous encounter with the

Green Knight. But he replied courteously to her teasing words.

She leaned over and kissed him, and he welcomed her warmly. Gazing at her, he thought how beautiful she looked.

"You see how I admire you," said the lady. "Tell me, do you love another, since you will not return my love?"

"I have no lady," replied Gawain with a smile.

"That is no comfort to me," sighed the lady, and she kissed him again.

"I know you are leaving soon, so I must say goodbye," she said. "Give me some token, by which I may remember you."

Gawain knew that if he gave her the smallest gift, it would signify that he had taken her as his lady and would compromise his honour as a knight. His reply was tactful so as to give no offence.

"Alas, I am a mere traveller, and have nothing to give which would be worthy of your beauty and reputation."

"If I am to receive no gift from you," she said, "at least accept this from me," and she offered him a ruby set in a rich gold ring.

Gawain knew that he could not accept such a compromising gift from a lady and quickly declined the jewel saying that he had nothing to offer in return.

"If you reject my ring," she said, "perhaps you would accept another gift, of no great value. Would you take my sash?"

Clasped round her waist was a sash of green silk with a golden hem.

Gawain was reluctant to accept any gift and again refused, but she continued to press him. "You are refusing such a small gift, yet although this sash seems worthless, it has magic properties and will protect any man from those who may try to kill him."

Gawain was silent. He pondered on his coming encounter with the Green Knight and thought how the girdle might save his life.

Seeing him hesitate, the lady pressed him the more, until at last Gawain accepted her gift. "But please," she begged, "do not let my husband know that I have given it to you." She embraced him for the third time, and then departed.

Gawain then got out of bed, dressed himself and went to church, where he confessed his sins and received absolution, thus he was well prepared for his encounter with the Green Knight.

The lord, continued his hunt for the fox, and spied the creature rushing through a hedge, pursued by the pack of hounds. The man drew his sword with cunning and drove at the fox but the beast leapt sideways, a dog bounded at him and the hunted animal fell in front of the horse's feet. All the dogs fell on him at once, tearing at his body. The great man dismounted speedily and lifted him out of reach of the dogs' fangs but the fox was torn to pieces.

The lord of the castle and his company returned home and found Gawain sitting before a roaring fire, dressed in a rich blue robe trimmed with ermine.

Gawain rose and went forward to greet the host.

"I will fulfil my part of the bargain first," he said, and embraced the man three times, but he kept quiet about his gift of the green girdle.

"Well," said the lord, "you seem to be getting the best of our bargain. Sadly, however, on this occasion, although I have hunted all day, I can only offer you this fox-pelt. It is a poor return for you."

"It is enough," said Gawain, and they went to supper.

As they parted for their evening's rest, Gawain thanked his host for his generous hospitality and begged him to supply the guide he had promised, to show him the way to the Green Chapel.

"With all my heart," said the host, and he gave instructions to a servant to conduct the knight on his journey the following morning.

Gawain again thanked the lord, and bade a graceful farewell to the two ladies. He felt sad, however, when he thought of the peril he was about to face at the Green Chapel.

So Gawain retired to bed, but his anxiety about the culmination of his adventure prevented him from sleeping easily. He had almost reached the end of his quest. Tomorrow he would know his destiny!

THE GREEN CHAPEL

NEW Year's Day approached, the weather was cold and blustery. The earth was covered with snow, and the bleak winds whistling round the stableyard made Gringolet shiver in his stall.

Gawain lay in bed early that morning, he had spent a restless night and was now wide awake, thinking of the great danger he was about to face that day.

Before dawn he rose and the servants brought him his newly burnished armour. He put on warm clothes beneath his breast-coat and wrapped his legs in the bright chain mail. He picked up the precious green girdle given to him by the lady. It would protect him from harm, she had said. He carefully tied it round his waist.

Gringolet was brought to him, the horse was glad to be moving at last, and looked fit and ready for battle. Gawain swung himself into the saddle, where his servant handed him his shield and spear. He was well prepared for his adventure, and rode out of the castle with a courteous farewell to the men and women he left behind. The guide provided by the lord of the castle accompanied him.

As he crossed the drawbridge, he saw in front of him a bare, desolate land of winter trees and cold rocks. Mist hung on the moors and snow covered the high mountains.

Gawain and his companion pressed forward until they reached a hill, where the guide reigned in his horse, he looked grave and solemn.

"You are not far from the place you seek, Sir Gawain, and you have shown true courage on your journey so far. I admire your bravery and courtesy so much that I want to warn you that you are heading towards a place of dire peril.

"The man you are destined to meet is brave and strong and mightier than any man on earth. He is far larger than any knight in King Arthur's Court. The Green Chapel is his dwelling place where no man has ever passed without losing his life. The giant shows no mercy, believe me. If you go on, you will certainly die, for no-one is a match for him. I beg you, therefore, to go home by another road, and I solemnly swear that I will return and say nothing about your flight."

"Thank you for your concern," replied the knight, "but however silent you were, although others may not know that I had run away, I would know that I had behaved like a coward.

"I will go to the Green Chapel to meet my fate. However fearsome this man is, I have faith in God, and He is strongest of all."

The guide sighed:

"I can see that you are determined to lose your life, so I will stand in your way no longer. Here is your lance and your helmet." He pointed ahead, "Ride down this path, and around that cliff until you reach a ravine. When you reach the valley, you will see the Green Chapel where the fierce man lives." He looked at the brave knight with sorrow and pity.

"Goodbye, Sir Gawain," he said, "I would not change places with you for all the money on earth." With these words, he turned his horse and rode off at great speed.

Gawain resolutely dug his spurs into Gringolet's side urging the horse down the path, to the ravine which the guide had pointed out to him. He searched about him, saw only hard, cruel rocks and barren land.

Then, far off, on a plain, he spied what seemed to be a fairy mound by the side of a stream. Gawain rode towards it and alighted from his horse so that he could approach more easily on foot.

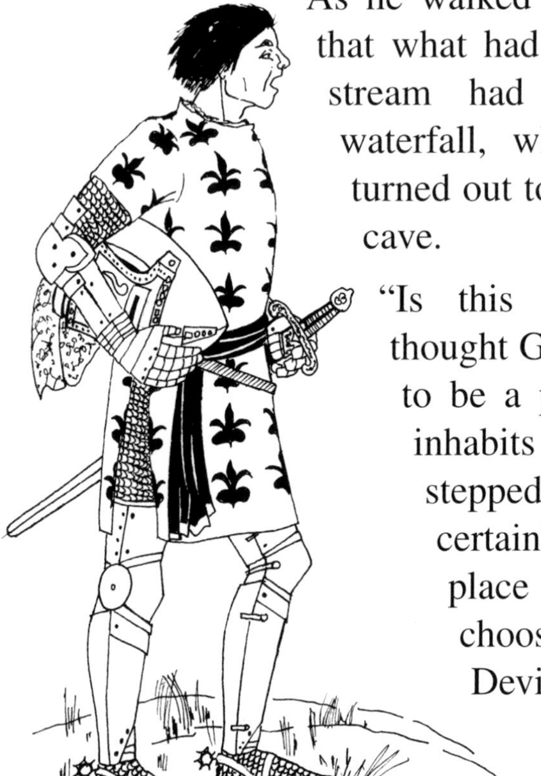

As he walked forward, he could see that what had seemed to him like a stream had become a whirling waterfall, while the fairy mound turned out to be nothing but an old cave.

"Is this the Green Chapel?" thought Gawain, "it seems to me to be a place which the Devil inhabits at dead of night." He stepped a little closer, "It is certainly deserted, just the place for the Green Man to choose. Perhaps he is the Devil himself, in disguise.

This certainly seems the most evil place I have ever entered." He shivered.

Gawain continued walking until he was on the top of the fairy mound. He stopped, looked and listened. He appeared to be quite alone. Then he listened again, more attentively. What was that sound? He could still see nothing and nobody. He listened again. Yes! There it was! A whirring and a whishing noise, as if someone were sharpening some huge piece of metal on a hard stone!

As Gawain listened, he felt his blood go cold, but he said to himself, bravely, "That terrible noise is meant to put fear in my heart, but I will not be afraid, even although I may be about to die!"

He called out boldly, (more boldly than he felt):

"Who lives here? Is anyone waiting here to meet me? I am Gawain, and I am ready for you."

He heard a voice from above him on the bank, it was stern and forceful, "Stay there, and you will receive the stroke I promised to give you last year, at King Arthur's Court."

Gawain waited, but the mysterious stranger still did not appear. The brave knight continued to hear the chilling, whirring noise he had heard previously. Then he realised what the huge man was doing. The Green Knight was sharpening his weapon, preparing to cut off Gawain's head!

Then, suddenly, the giant appeared from behind a great rock. He towered above Gawain and he held in his hand the huge, terrible axe, shining and newly sharpened, its blade was four foot wide with a fine cutting edge! Here then was the Green Knight, ready to exact the promise given to him a year ago in the court of King Arthur!

The big man was dressed in green as he had been a year ago, when Gawain had accepted his challenge and had struck off the giant's head.

Gawain saw that he had the same long green hair and green bushy beard, only this time he was not seated on the great green horse but he stood on the ground. The green man vaulted over the stream, using his axe to help him and strode towards Gawain. He was grim and threatening. Gawain took a few steps towards him and faced his adversary, but on this occasion the good knight did not offer him the courteous bow he had given him at their previous meeting.

They stood facing each other. The Green Knight stared at Gawain. "You have kept your bargain on time, as a true knight should," he boomed. "Twelve months ago, you struck off my head, now it is my turn." His voice was stern. "Take off your helmet, and bare your head. It is time to receive your payment. You must stand as meekly as I did when you cut off my head with one stroke."

"By the God who made me," said Gawain firmly, "I stand by our bargain. Strike the blow and I will stand still to receive it, I swear."

Gawain bent forward to expose his neck, nor did he show any fear, although he trembled in his heart.

Then the Green Knight gathered his weapon, raised it high above his head, ready to swing it down heavily on Gawain's neck.

But the noble knight could not help glancing up, and seeing that fearsome shining blade, he hunched up his shoulders as he waited for the sharp axe to descend on his bare neck.

When the man saw this slight movement, he stayed his axe and mocked Gawain:

"You are supposed to be so brave that an army would not frighten you. Yet now you flinch from fear even before you feel anything. I did not expect such cowardice. I did not flinch from you when you struck me. My head fell to the floor, but I did not run away. Yet you cower with fright even before you have received any harm. I am surely the better and braver man."

"I shall not shrink again," Gawain was mortified, "even if my head is severed from my body. But be quick about it, do what you have to do. I swear I shall take your blow without flinching."

"Here it comes then," said the other, raising the axe angrily.

Gawain stood patiently, his neck bent forward. He heard the weapon descend, then unaccountably, the man held back, and offered no blow. Gawain waited unflinchingly, as still as a stone.

Then the Green Knight whirled the axe round and prepared to strike again. He lifted the axe high above his head:

"May the chivalry of King Arthur's Court preserve you and save your neck," he said.

"Get on with it, stop boasting," said Gawain, "you speak fiercely, but I believe you are a coward yourself."

"I will stay no more," said the huge man, and prepared to strike the third time.

Gawain was full of grief, nothing could save him now.

Up went the axe, and swung down towards his bare neck, but though it descended heavily, as this third blow reached his neck, the weapon slowed down in flight and made only a slight wound, a little nick on the white flesh.

Where the skin was broken, blood spurted to the ground.

When Gawain saw his blood on the snow, he leapt away, donned his helmet, placed his shield in front of him and drew his bright sword:

"Strike me no more, you can offer no more blows unchallenged," he said to the Green Knight, "I have sustained the one blow, as I promised, if you offer another I shall retaliate with my own weapon."

The Green Man stood still and leaned on his axe, gazing at Gawain. "What a bold and courageous knight!" thought the big man. "What a truly great warrior!"

"Brave knight, do not be so warlike," he said, "no-one has done evil to you. The bargain made at King Arthur's Court has been kept here today.

I am also the lord who entertained you at my castle, but you did not recognise my disguise.

"You remember we struck three bargains, when you should give me whatever you received in the castle and I would give you what I had won in the hunt. When my lady visited you in your room, you were tempted three times. You were then in the greatest peril. If you had not resisted these temptations, you would have lost your life here at the Green Chapel.

"The first time I raised my axe, I pretended to strike you but did not, because you kept your vow in the castle after the first hunt. You remember, you gave me the one embrace you had received from the lady in exchange for the deer I had caught and killed in the hunt.

"I raised my axe a second time but did not strike the blow, because you also kept your promise a second time when you embraced me twice as my lady had done with you. In exchange I gave you the wild boar I had killed in the hunt.

"When my lady visited you the third time, you were unable to wholly resist the tempting offer of the green girdle, which she said would save your life. You concealed that gift from me, when you gave me only the three embraces you had received from the lady. Thus my third blow nicked your flesh.

"I knew everything that was happening in the castle while I was away hunting. It was I who sent the lady to tempt you, and you behaved courteously at all times. Even though you gave in to the temptation of the green girdle, you did so not for worldly gain, you had refused the rich jewel offered to you. You could not resist the green girdle because you love life, for which no one can blame you. You may think if you wish that the green girdle really did offer you some protection."

For a long time Gawain stood in silence. He felt very angry at the deceptions practised on him, but he was ashamed of his one failure, in being tempted to accept the green girdle as a gift.

Finally the brave knight spoke.

"The sins of greed and cowardice are the downfall of many virtuous men." He felt his failure keenly. He tore the girdle from his waist and thrust it angrily at the Green Knight.

"That is my falsehood and my shame. I took it because I am a coward. I shall always be considered by my fellow knights to be fearful, treacherous and unchivalrous. I am utterly miserable and griefstricken at my failure to uphold the honour of the great king Arthur, as I promised. I would like your permission to leave this place as quickly as possible."

The other man smiled, "Your very words demonstrate how fit you are to represent the chivalry of King Arthur's Court, yours was such a small fault. You showed immense courage when you faced the prospect of certain death at my hands, so you may leave here as pure of sin as the day you were born.

"As for the green girdle, take it, Sir Gawain, it will remind you of your great adventure." The Green Knight paused. He continued, "You will always be welcome at my castle, especially at Christmas time."

"Remember me to your lady," replied Gawain, putting on his helmet. "I shall take the girdle, but I shall wear it to remind me of my sin, and of my human failing." Gawain took the sash from the Green Knight and tied it once more round his waist.

He looked curiously at his former adversary. “Tell me, before I depart, what is your real name?”

“My name is Bertilak,” the big man replied, “I am not the bad fellow you may think. You may recall an old woman sitting beside my lady in church. She was the enchantress Morgan le Fey, in disguise. You know that it is she who means to thwart her cousin Arthur at every opportunity. She cast a spell on me and mine and caused me to behave as I did. She bewitched me and my lady, but your courtesy, honour and bravery have triumphed over her evil. You have done us good service also.”

When Gawain heard this he was astounded. Again, he thanked the Green Knight, and took his leave. Thus, the two men parted and went their separate ways.

When Gawain returned home to the court of King Arthur, he told everyone of his amazing adventure, and of his great shame at accepting the gift of the green girdle.

King Arthur and the Knights of the Round Table listened carefully to Gawain’s tale and when he had finished speaking they were silent for a while. They thought of the honourable way he had behaved throughout all the dangers he had faced. At last Arthur rose to his feet. He looked around at the companions of the Round Table, Launcelot, Kay, Bedivere, and his own nephew, Gawain, looking somewhat ashamed.

"My friends," said the king, "I think you will agree that Gawain's adventure has been truly miraculous. He has borne himself with courage and courtesy as a true knight of the Round Table. He feels some shame because he accepted the green girdle." Gawain's colour rose. I believe he acted as my true champion, and he has my love and gratitude for his behaviour."

Launcelot rose to his feet. "Friends," he said, "I believe I speak for all, when I say that we heartily agree with our great and beloved king. Furthermore, I would like to suggest that henceforth, we should all wear a similar green girdle to remind us always of the amazing story of Sir Gawain and the Green Knight."

With this all the knights agreed.